Partially Broken Never Destroyed 6

Unfinished Business

Nataisha T. Hill

Published by TaiLorMade Books

Chapter 1

About two months had passed since Bryan was released from the hospital. Kayla was now four months into her pregnancy and things were tense at home. Although Kayla would try to be supportive in Bryan's recovery, her mood swings were beyond horrific. There would be times that she'd come home from work crying, laughing, or pissed off all in the same week. To make matters worse, Bryan was ready to return to his job, but his physician hadn't issued his release papers. Being that the bullet had penetrated from his back to his chest, doctors wanted to be sure he was properly healing. They explained that any work he did for the next six months would need to be light duty and no standing for long periods of time.

Unfortunately for Bryan, being at home all day was making him fall into a depressive state. He needed something to help take his mind off the death of Wayne, who was his best man. His boss Alex had told him that the investigators said it was an early morning drive-by shooting outside of a local bar. They believed that Wayne went outside to smoke or use his phone. Police believed that Wayne was hit with some sort of silencer since no one complained or heard of any gunshots. Apparently, there weren't any known witnesses to come forward, which would prolong the investigation. Bryan didn't ask Alex too many questions about what he knew. His deeper fear was what Kayla had told him about the family huddle in the hospital. His family speaking in French raised suspicions and resurrected a haunting past that he thought was buried. For the sake of his new family, he prayed it would remain that way.

Meanwhile, back at the hospital, a few changes were made for Kayla. She had her own private office and she was now in charge of giving out the errands. Her new team seemed to be just as excited about her pregnancy as she was. She had been putting off the ultrasound until Bryan got well, but she finally made an appointment and things seemed to be going good. That is, everything except for Meg's nuisance.

Meg was still walking around free but was clearly spiraling out of control and blaming Kayla for it. She'd send Kayla flowers at least twice a week with an attached note hinting for Kayla to get rid of the video. On top of that, she would do strange things such as follow Kayla to the cafeteria during lunch or leave at the same time when Kayla would leave for the day.

Kayla had begun to feel like Meg was daring her to turn in the video. Kayla was hoping that investigators would catch Meg, so she wouldn't have to deal with it period. She wasn't sure if the police even considered Meg as a suspect. She figured the detectives were probably too busy focusing on any of Jared's dissatisfied clients or people who lost cases against him. The bottom line was that Kayla was getting sick of Meg. Instead of releasing the video to the authorities, Kayla considered sending an anonymous copy to Dylan Wright, Meg's husband who was also Jared's secret lover.

"Hey Boo Boo! Have I told you how happy I am that you're back, all glowin' and stuff?" Dexter said, walking into Kayla's office and sitting on the edge of her desk.

"Dexter, sit down in the chair like a normal person. I don't know where your booty was last night," Kayla chuckled.

Although Dexter was messy, he always seemed to have Kayla's back. He constantly brought her little gifts for the baby and would give her all the juicy updates about any drama going on in the hospital. He still despised Meg and would purposely go talk to Kayla before Meg could approach her. Kayla couldn't give him all the details of what was going on with Meg, but she did tell Dexter that Meg was blaming her for getting arrested at her wedding.

"I can't tell you where it was last night because the baby might hear me and come out calling me nasty Nay Nay, okay?" he responded.

Kayla laughed hysterically, "What's going on, Boo?"

"Girrrl, let me close this door...because I got some tea for you, bitch."

5

"Speaking of which, I know you use the word 'bitch' as words of endearment, but you have to break the habit. These snitches around here have been complaining."

"Jealous hoes complain because I put them hoes to shame, okay?" I got something on all these hatin' hoes and they betta know it."

Kayla shook her head and asked, "What's the tea boo?"

"Guess who's pregnant."

"Uhh...," Kayla said, looking down at her stomach.

"How come you always gotta be funny? No Boo, Meg is pregnant."

"Dexter, you got ten seconds to get the hell out of my office."

"What? I'm serious. This old scalawag is pregnant."

"First off, Meg is like fifty and probably has gone through menopause already, so what creature crawled out of hell and whispered that lie to you?"

"Well, I guess she paid money to take them old eggs through some type of restoration program, because I mess with Bobby and Bobby has a first cousin named Donny, who is Meg's new boo thang."

"I'm assuming that Donny is a black man, which is already forbidden in Meg's 'high society' and is yet another reason why I'm not believing this story."

"Well, he kinda light skinned with good hair, so maybe she thought he was Dominican Republican or some. Girl, I don't know. All I know is that he been dumping that thang like Oreo cookies in milk, okay?"

—

"Why did Donny confide in Bobby about all of this?"

"Girl, Bobby don't really care for Donny, but Donny and Bobby's momma are close. Bobby said he was ova his momma house and he overheard Donny talking about how he got this rich, married woman pregnant. Bobby didn't think too much of it until Donny said that the woman worked at Fairview Hospital. Girl, my baby stood by that door and got all that tea."

"I'm still not believing it, Dexy. Perhaps Donny was just trying to see if Bobby would run his mouth to you or something, so you can go back and tell Meg."

"Girl, Donny doesn't know me and has even less knowing of where I work. Bobby and Donny don't even talk to each other anymore. Donny cut Bobby off when he announced he was gay."

"What tha fuck?" Kayla said, completely astounded.

Dexter started laughing, "I knew you still had that ghetto in you, Boo."

"I still don't understand how all this could be possible."

"Uhh…the bitch probably saw the biggest penis she'd ever seen and spread eagle. What do you mean how is it possible?"

"That's not what I mean, Simpleton, but allow me to humor you for a minute and say that Meg is pregnant. What makes Donny think he is the father and not her husband or somebody else?"

"Girl, if you don't stop with yo foolishness," he laughed. "You and I both know that Mr. Wright been shooting blanks for decades and who else you know would want that old hag?"

Kayla didn't respond. Despite the fact that Dexter hated Meg, she was very attractive for her age. Kayla knew she couldn't tell Dexter about Meg's illicit affair with Jared, who Meg actually murdered two months ago, so she had to let him win the argument.

"Oops, I just got paged. I'ma go make these rounds real quick and I'll be back," Dexter said, immediately leaving.

Kayla sat there still unnerved about Meg possibly being pregnant. *This tea couldn't possibly be true* she thought. There had to have been some mix up in names or miscommunication somewhere. The hospital was huge and there were plenty of women named Meg that worked there. Perhaps Dexter's boyfriend had mistaken Meg's identity. Nevertheless, it would help to explain Meg's awkward behavior and desperation to get rid of the video. Furthermore, Meg being pregnant would only intensify her desperation, putting Kayla right back in the middle of harms way. Kayla had to find a way to validate these claims. She sat there thinking about several possibilities and scenarios that could play out if all this was true. It became apparent to her that she was the only woman in the world who had a boss that killed her ex lover, who was also her husband's lover. Now to top it all off, this maniac could possibly be pregnant by an entirely different man.

"Good morning Mrs. Phillips," said one of Dr. Roberts's assistants, interrupting Kayla's thoughts.

Kayla had chosen Dr. Roberts and Dr. Thomas for her obstetricians. She had established a business relationship with both doctors and was a fan of their work. Besides, who was better to take care of her than the people she had known for years.

—

"Hello Jennifer, how are you?" Kayla asked, motioning for her to enter.

"Oh, I just stopped by to give you this note from Dr. Roberts."

Kayla noticed that Jennifer seemed nervous as she handed her the envelope. She assumed that Jennifer already knew what it said since she did all of Dr. Roberts's paperwork. As quickly as she walked in, she hurriedly walked out of the office. Kayla immediately opened the note and read it. She couldn't believe her eyes as she felt tears beginning to form. Dr. Roberts was apologizing for not being able to continue to be her obstetrician. Kayla was extremely emotional, and she needed answers. As she grabbed her things to promptly go and pay Dr. Roberts a personal visit, she tried to calm herself as much as possible. Deep down she knew this had to be the demonic work of Meg Wright, who was also long-time friends with Dr. Roberts.

Chapter 2

While sitting at home with Nicholas watching cartoons, Bryan received a phone call from Alex. He had been hoping for the last few weeks that Alex would take the initiative to reach out to him. Alex informed Bryan that his doctor had faxed over all the release papers, so he could return to work whenever he was ready. Bryan was so thrilled that he agreed to meet Alex to discuss new planning; momentarily forgetting that he had Nicholas. He didn't want to call Alex back to cancel, and it would be at least another four hours before Kayla arrived home. He called his mom, Irene who happily agreed to watch Nicholas while he tended to his business.

After arriving at Ms Irene's home, Nicholas was instructed to sit down on the couch and watch television while Bryan talked to Ms. Irene in the kitchen. Oddly, she hadn't been around much after his hospital release like Bryan assumed she would have. Although Kayla was there for him, she could only do so much. Kayla was partially handicap by default and she worked in the daytime. He wasn't sure if his ordeal traumatized his mom or if there was something unrelated going on with her, but he needed to know if everything was okay.

"Hey momma. What's going on with you?"

"Nothing much. I'm just surviving by the grace of God."

"I haven't been seeing or hearing from you much. Is everything good?"

"Boy, you know where I am. I rarely ever change my routine. I've been making things for my grand baby and waiting on her arrival."

"See momma that's how I know we're out of touch. We didn't tell you the baby is a girl. We haven't even gone to the ultrasound doctor."

"Boy, you don't need a doctor when God's your advisor. Besides, your cousins have been running me up the wall with all their problems. I don't have time for anything else."

"Momma, you don't need to involve yourself with their issues. They are grown, and they need to start figuring things out for themselves."

"Son, everyone is not as well off as you and they need help and general guidance."

"What kind of help? I know they better not be asking you for money."

"Son, this is not a good time to talk about this, okay? I want you to go to your meeting, so you can do what you need to do to take care of my new grand baby."

Bryan knew his mom was hiding something, but he didn't want to press the issue. Anytime she got involved with his cousins' problems, they were either begging for money or someone wanted her to keep their kids for an uncertain amount of time. They never repaid his mom or send money for their kids the entire time she has them. Bryan was fed up and wasn't having it. After his meeting with Alex, he was going to get to the bottom of the secret his mom was keeping.

Alex's car was already parked in the back of the business complex by the time Bryan arrived. Bryan knew that Alex kept the back door locked for security purposes, so he used his key to a private entrance on the side. Once he walked in the door, he heard Alex's voice from a back room. He didn't want to make it seem as if he was eavesdropping, so he went to the back for his presence to be acknowledged. Alex was turned around in his chair, facing the wall as if he had already heard Bryan, but wanted privacy. Respecting his implied wishes, Bryan went up to the front to hang out until Alex was done with his call. Hearing Alex in a heated conversation just helped him to realize how everyone around him had their own set of problems.

It was almost noon, so the front of the parking lot was full of people coming and going to surrounding stores to help keep Bryan distracted. While looking out, Bryan saw a kid about 30 yards away fall on the concrete. Just as he opened the glass door to go out and help, the child's mother ran to his aid. He was relieved that the child wasn't hurt as he watched the mother fasten him in his seatbelt. As Bryan continued to look in their direction, he saw strange movements through their car window from the car beside them. The mother must have noticed too, because she quickly buckled herself in and pulled off.

Bryan thought his eyes were deceiving him as he quickly recognized the driver. Jesse was on the phone, banging her fist against her steering wheel as if she had gone mad. *What the fuck is she doing on our lot*, he thought. Everyone thought she had skipped town since she didn't show up to Wayne's funeral. Was she stalking him? Did someone send her to kill Wayne and now him? Bryan quickly became paranoid as he felt a panic attack about to ensue. He slowly stepped away from the door, hoping she didn't see him. Suddenly, Jesse quickly sped off, almost side swiping another car.

"I'm sorry about that," Alex said, startling Bryan from behind. "What's wrong man? You act like you've seen a ghost."

Bryan just stood there unable to gather his thoughts. He couldn't figure out what had just happened. Jesse speeds out of the parking lot and then Alex suddenly comes up front. Was this a coincidence or was there something seriously going on with them? Perhaps his mind was playing tricks on him.

Alex seemed as if he was happily married with a daughter on the way. Why would Alex jeopardize what he had going on with a thot like Jesse? Bryan decided that perhaps he was thinking too much into the matter. Maybe it wasn't Jesse at all. People can look alike from a distance. Although the car was similar to Jesse's car, it was parked at another store and she didn't even look in their direction when she left. Bryan shook his head and let it go.

"Man, I'm just stressed. I've been recovering, out of work, and a baby on the way. At times I don't know my left hand from my right hand," Bryan admitted.

"Oh, I'm right here with you, man. You know my wife is scheduled to deliver in about two months, so basically, I need you in control of everything."

"That's why I'm here," Bryan said, following Alex to the back office.

"I know things are going to be different without Wayne," mentioned Alex in a solemn tone.

"Yeah, I still can't believe it, man. One minute he is handing me a champagne bottle, the next minute I'm shot, and a day later he's dead."

"That is the craziest shit I've ever heard," Alex said, quickly removing an object from the top of his cabinet, tossing it into his desk drawer. "Speaking of which, have you heard from Jesse?"

"Have I heard from Jesse? Of course not, what made you ask me that?"

"Oh...uh...nothing," Alex stammered, "just thought that she might try to give you some of his belongings from his house, that's all."

"I think Wayne's dad took care of it. How many upcoming properties do we have?" Bryan asked, pretending to shrug off his suspicions about Alex.

It was right then that Bryan realized he wasn't delusional, but he wasn't going to press the issue at that particular moment. All that stuttering and shit while bringing up Jesse's name had him thinking. When in the hell did Alex get to know Jesse on a first name basis? She wasn't at the funeral and even when he was alive, Wayne never mentioned to him that Jesse and Alex had met. Sure, Jesse brought Wayne lunch, but Alex was hardly ever at the job site once he gave out the blueprints. Bryan knew it had to have been Jesse in the parking lot and he had a good feeling that she wasn't there to spy on him. Jesse had pulled up because she was there for Alex.

Chapter 3

Kayla walked up to Dr. Robert's office and stood at the door. He was on the phone, but she decided to stay there and wait since her concern was urgent. She was under the impression that she and Dr. Roberts were close enough to at least discuss the matter face to face before just dropping her. She waved at him through the window to get his attention. He looked up and motioned for her to enter as he ended his phone call. She walked in the room and he greeted Kayla with a smile and a warm handshake as if nothing had happened.

"Hello, Kayla. What brings you by here? Are you okay? Our appointment isn't until this Friday."

"I was aware and looking forward to it until I got this letter," she responded, handing it to him.

"Oh, wow!" he stated, reading the letter as if it was new to him.

"Kayla, I'm sorry, but I didn't expect this."

"What do you mean? You didn't write it?"

"Well, it's complicated. You see, sometimes the board will decide whether it's in our best interest to affiliate obstetrician services to its members, or if there is a priority case, we must consider that case first. It appears as if your situation suits the second scenario."

"I don't get it. I'm also on the board under Meg. Don't I get a vote?"

"You do, but as you stated, you are under Meg."

Kayla worse fears were confirmed. Meg's ancient ass must really have been pregnant. Meg also must have written the letter and had Jennifer deliver it, knowing that Dr. Roberts would comply. Kayla wasn't going to allow Meg to steal her doctor. She was going to plead her case by any means.

"Listen Dr. Roberts. I know everything that's going on with Meg. I definitely understand that you have the obligation of looking out for her first, but I will not be a bother if you can also remain my doctor."

"You mean you already know?"

"Yes, I am aware of everything."

Dr. Roberts got up and closed the blinds in the office windows. The doors were already shut, so no one was able to hear him. Was Meg's pregnancy such a secret that he was afraid someone would read his lips? His behavior seemed very bizarre over a pregnancy.

"Kayla, I don't want you to think I'm a bad person."

"Of course not, I understand Dr. Roberts. You are a man of good character, so you have to do what you have to do to keep the people around you content."

"Thank you, Kayla. I really appreciate that. I obviously didn't expect something like this to happen. You'd be surprised to know that several of our fellow colleagues have also experienced their one night of carelessness. Don't get me wrong. It doesn't make it okay by any means, but we all are human, and we make mistakes."

One night of carelessness thought Kayla? *If only Dr. Roberts knew how big of a whore Meg was, he'd have her vagina checked daily.*

"Dr. Roberts, I can assure you that even Meg herself didn't expect this to happen, but we all have to deal with the curves that life sometimes throws us."

"Well said, Kayla. I just wish it would be this easy explaining this to my wife. I didn't think I could even have any more kids at my age."

Kayla swallowed hard, trying not to react to what Dr. Roberts had just admitted. Even though she had to pretend like the information wasn't new to her, Dr. Roberts had just dropped the biggest bombshell she could have ever imagined. Dr. Roberts smashed the trash! It was obvious that he assumed Meg had already confided in her since everyone assumed that she was Meg's protégé. Although Meg had nice physical qualities, no one seemed to recognize the evilness that existed within her. This woman had to have a super pussy or the best head a head could give. Of all people, she would never expect Dr. Roberts to get caught in her twisted web. He was a decent man from what Kayla knew and she couldn't just allow him to drown in Meg's treachery.

19

"Well, Dr. Roberts, I didn't want to get in the middle of things, but just as a precaution, perhaps you should hold off on mentioning the pregnancy in your confession to your wife until the results are conclusive."

"Do you think I really should?"

"Well, I'm assuming that you love your wife and plan to stay married, correct?"

"Of course, I do. My wife and I have been married for over twenty years and I still love her dearly."

"Okay, I'm sure it will be easier to explain a moment of weakness opposed to a lifetime of raising a kid that you're not certain is yours."

"I understand what you are saying, but Meg is a great woman and I've known her for a long time. She admitted that I was the only other man she'd slept with in the past fifteen years since she first started dating Dylan. He's a great guy, too. They've been unable to have kids and in my one night of drunkenness, sob stories, and thinking with my manhood, I pulled the trigger. Kayla, this is hard to admit, but I messed up and I am truly ashamed."

Kayla had to hold her head down to pretend she was coughing to prevent herself from hysterically laughing in Dr. Roberts's face. Meg was not only conniving, but she was hilarious. She couldn't believe that Meg had told this man that he was the only man she'd been with in fifteen years. It was probably more like fifteen hours. Kayla didn't want to believe that Dr. Roberts was this naive. What was she telling all the other suckers she had caught up in her deceit?

Kayla wanted nothing more than to let Dr. Roberts know that Meg was a compulsive liar and a con-artist. She wanted him to know how his possible baby momma-to-be just eliminated one of her possibilities indefinitely. Unfortunately, she couldn't. The only proof that Kayla had of Meg's hellish rein was the video. Kayla was afraid for the safety of her and her unborn child if she released it. In the mist of Meg's psychotic ways, she always seemed to have at least one conspirator on deck that was willing to do her dirty work. If it wasn't for the threat that Kayla had made of an anonymous source releasing the video should something happen to her, Meg would have surely tried to kill her by now.

"I understand Dr. Roberts, but all I'm saying is that you also thought you were too old to have kids. Perhaps you are." Kayla reasoned, after gaining her composure.

"I guess you're right about that, too. I could just wait and make sure the baby is biracial," he added.

Kayla waited to see if he was joking before responding. Dr. Roberts seemed to have a positive outlook despite his infidelity, however he had no earthly idea of the danger that this situation presented. Meg was lying to everyone regarding her circumstances and Kayla began to doubt if she was even pregnant. It wasn't that hard to get a hold of someone else's positive pregnancy test in their line of work. Even if Meg was expecting, there was no way she would know who fathered that child. She seduced the good doctor, cut her ex-lover's throat, and there was no telling what type of guy this Donny character was. Meg's husband would be the only guy to exclude in this twisted debauchery.

"Dr. Roberts, I know you and I hadn't personally spoken about this, and now I see things from a different perspective. I'm okay with another recommendation due to the circumstances."

As Kayla walked out of Dr. Roberts's office, she was left feeling tired and depleted. Her goal was to be as far away from Meg as possible. She decided from that point forward, she was going to apply for a position at a private practice and eventually start one of her own. Meg had another thing coming if she thought she was going to get some sympathy from Kayla for a pregnancy that may not even exist. Besides, Meg was the furthest thing from a positive mother figure and was incapable of being a stable parent. Kayla needed more information from Dexter about Donny. He just might be the only person willing to put Meg in her place.

Chapter 4

After the meeting with Alex was over, Bryan took his time
before returning to his mom's house. He couldn't help but to think
about the bizarre incident that had taken place. Although he didn't
mention Wayne or Jesse the remaining time there, the elephant in the
room stood big and tall. Jesse cheating on Wayne was no surprise,
but Wayne ending up dead while his girlfriend is sitting outside of
his boss's business all hysterical two months later had arisen several
questions. Bryan figured had Alex been talking to his wife, that's the
first thing he would have mentioned once he walked up front. Based
on how thrilled he was to be off work while his wife had the baby, it
didn't sound like Alex was beefing with his wife. Furthermore,
Bryan had never heard Alex use that tone of voice with his wife.

Based on the evidence that he put together, Alex smashed Jesse, she wants more, and Alex is trying to disappear for a while, but why? How deep was their involvement? Bryan didn't give a damn if Alex was smashing or not for the most part. It was lowdown, but there were other pressing issues. Did Alex get so caught up that he had something to do with Wayne's death? Did Jesse act alone to show her loyalty to Alex or were they both in on it? Alex was obviously his bread and butter, but he wasn't willing to work for someone who helped to get his best friend killed. If anything, he was hoping Jesse acted alone, so her ass could rot in prison.

It was around five in the evening when Bryan arrived back at his mom's house and Nicholas was napping. Bryan didn't feel like dealing with issues within his family now that he discovered issues at work. He went to the back to thank his mom and tell her bye.

"Momma, what's wrong?" He asked, seeing Ms. Irene wipe her face.

"Oh, hi son. I didn't here you come in?"

"Why are you crying, momma? What's going on?"

"I'm not crying. You know good and well I have allergies, boy."

"If I call Renee or Jon Junior, is that what they're going to tell me?"

"You asked me a question and I gave you my answer. Take Nicholas home, take care of your wife, and pray before you go to sleep."

"Momma, I'm not six. What are you talking about? Stop trying to speak in parables and tell me what's going on."

"Jesus spoke in parables, son."

"I'll talk to Jesus later. I'm about to call Jon Junior and see what you're not telling me."

"Jon Junior not there, son."

"He has a cell phone that can go anywhere he can."

"Jon Junior is gone away for a while. He won't be able to answer."

"Oh, so Jon Junior is in jail again and wants bail money, huh? Nope, we're not getting him out of jail again, Momma."

"Son, sometimes you need to let things go and do as you're told. Now, I haven't asked you for a damn dime, have I?

"Momma, you never ask me directly for the bail money, but it's the same thing when I have to give you money for utilities or groceries."

"Well next time let me burn candles and eat sardines with crackers." She responded.

Bryan was furious and didn't want to continue the argument with his mom. He gave her a quick kiss on the cheek before grabbing Nicholas and leaving the house. He was appalled that his cousins were still asking his mom for money after all that she had been through. He decided to wait until Nicholas wasn't around to have the conversation he planned to have with Jon Junior or anybody else who thought that his mom was their personal ATM.

Kayla wasn't home yet, so Bryan decided to go ahead and put chicken in the oven for dinner. Nicholas went to his room to play his special ops game, which gave Bryan time to handle his family business. Renee and Jon Junior were not only first cousins, but they were like brother and sister. Renee knew any and everything that was going on with him and vice-versa. Since talking to Jon Junior would be like talking to a brick wall, he decided to call Renee instead.

"What's going on Nee Nee?" Bryan asked as she answered.

"I hope you're calling to apologize for the way you acted at the reception," she answered.

"Girl, I almost died. Do you think I give a damn about that weak ass situation? Besides, you had no right to disrespect me and my wife on our wedding day. Who does that?"

"Well, hooray for Bryan. At least you still got someone to marry. My baby daddy is locked up, remember?"

"Man, I can't believe that you're still buggin' off that. That grown ass man made his own decisions. I told him it was a setup, he didn't listen, and now he's suffering the consequences."

"No, I'm suffering the consequences, Bryan. I lost my baby and my man."

Bryan held the phone for a minute, regretting that he called her. He didn't understand how she was unable to move on after almost six years. He knew if he continued to say how he really felt that he would get nowhere. He had to switch his approach and try a different strategy.

"At the end of the day we're family, Renee. You and I used to be even closer than you and Jon Junior. I personally wouldn't mind getting back to the way it was. How about you, me, Jon Junior, and all the first cousins get together at the end of this month and do something as a family?"

"That may be okay if you're paying," she apathetically responded.

"I'll pay for the women, but the guys have to hold their own."

"Well, everybody ain't got it like you Bryan, and I don't know if Jon Junior is coming."

"Why not?" Bryan asked, leading her exactly where he wanted her to go.

"Oh…Irene didn't tell you that you have a family debt with Jon Junior?"

"What? I don't owe that nigga shit. I haven't been around Jon Junior in at least two years and he still owe me for bailing him out last time."

"Who said anything about you having to bail him out? Jon Junior isn't even in jail."

"Well, what in the hell are we even talking about right now?"

"It's a crime damn shame that even after all this time you're still oblivious about who calls the shots. If your wife hadn't ran her mouth about who called who that day, none of this would have happened."

Bryan immediately hung up the phone and had to sit down from what he heard. His life had become that much more chaotic. It didn't take a rocket scientist to comprehend what Renee was trying to say. It was now obvious to Bryan what his mom couldn't tell him. Someone in his family must have been under the impression that Wayne tried to kill him. In actuality, Bryan didn't know who pulled the trigger. Of course, Jesse shouldn't have had the gun in the first place, but Bryan figured it was an accident. Things were different when he assumed that Jesse and Alex could have been involved in Wayne's murder, but Renee had put an unimaginable spin on things. How was he going to deal with his family possibly killing his best man for no reason?

Chapter 5

After her visit with Dr. Roberts, Kayla was too drained to return to her office. She decided that getting Dexter in the middle of things was too risky. Dexter was known for switching men about as often as he switched his iPhone playlists, so she didn't want anything involving him to backfire. Besides, as much as Dexter hated Meg, Kayla knew that he would be gathering anything against her that he could without even being asked. Her new plan was to sit tight and allow Dexter to be Dexter and figure out a different strategy to get information about Meg. Once Kayla had gotten to her car, she noticed a missed call from an unknown number and a message. She pressed play to listen and was shocked at the least.

Hello, Kayla. This is Dylan. I first want to apologize for my actions regarding the incident a while back. You didn't deserve what I put you through and I'm deeply sorry. You were always kind and I enjoyed our friendship. Without saying too much, I am at a lost and I need your assistance. Could you please do an old friend a favor and meet me some where, so we can talk? It would truly mean a lot. Thank you.

After listening to the message three times, Kayla still couldn't figure out Dylan's motive. He should have been sorry long before he left this message, so why the apology now? Did he know about Meg's alleged pregnancy? Was Meg also telling him that his sperm magically worked after all these years? Dylan was obviously trying to get whatever information he assumed she had about his wife, but Kayla wasn't having it. He had lost his damn mind if he thought for one minute that he was going to swindle any information from her.

On the other hand, she couldn't ignore the fact that she was curious to know what was Dylan so lost about and why he couldn't discuss it over the phone. Could his grief stem from Jared's death? She did recall how Jared confided in depth with her regarding his love affair with Dylan and how deeply in love they were with each other.

According to Jared, Dylan shot his wife only because she was stealing from their bank account, not because he found out that Meg was having an affair. Jared claimed that Dylan didn't have any affectionate feelings towards Meg, which didn't make sense to her. There had to have been some type of feelings involved or else he wouldn't have shot at Kayla.

30

Kayla originally assumed that Dylan was upset with her from thinking she helped to hide Meg's affair, but perhaps he shot at her because he didn't want any witnesses. Either way, Dylan reaching out to her was strange. However, against her better judgment, she decided to entertain Dylan's proposal. She called him and agreed to meet him at the same downtown restaurant that Jared had taken her to. She hoped that he wouldn't be psycho enough to pull something in public in front of familiar faces and his colleagues.

Kayla still had about an hour or so before she was expected home, so she didn't call to tell Bryan about her unexpected meeting. She called the restaurant in advance for seating and they were glad to accommodate her. Having had Jared as an attorney had definitely came with its perks. Once Kayla had arrived and walked into the candlelit entrance, the hostess checked her name and apologized regarding Jared's untimely death. The hostess had also advised her that her reservations had been changed and escorted her to a "members' suite" area. Dylan obviously saw her reservation and trumped it with his own. She wasn't sure if this was an intimidation tactic, but she reluctantly went along with it.

The members' suite was spacious and quite impressive. In the middle of the room was a huge chandelier and the tables had cloths that were designed with luxurious linens and crystal swan centerpieces. It was no surprise that he had booked the entire suite.

"I'm so glad you could make it, Kayla," Mr. Wright said, standing up to greet Kayla with a hug.

She didn't want to seem stand-offish, so she embraced him with a light tap.

"I know you're probably not my biggest fan right now, so I honestly and sincerely appreciate you coming. I hope you're not offended, but I took the liberty of upgrading our seating to something more comfortable and private."

"No offense taken. It's good to see that you're doing okay after everything that has happened. I'm sorry that you guys lost a great friend."

Kayla wasn't sure if Dylan was aware of what Jared had confessed to her, so for now, she was going to choose her words carefully.

"Jared was definitely a great friend and he will be dearly missed. How are things going with you? Meg tells me you have your own office now."

Kayla had enough of this cookie-cutter conversation. They weren't on good terms, so she didn't understand why he continued to talk as if they were still good friends. Memories of her diving into bushes to dodge his bullets suddenly resurfaced. Kayla's friendliness was fading as quickly as his fake hairline.

"Meg tells me you two are divorcing because of your relationship with Jared."

"Wow! Okay. I definitely didn't expect that, but I can appreciate your directness," he admitted, taking a drink. "I took the liberty of ordering us some champagne."

"No thank you. My fetus wouldn't like it."

"Oh, I didn't know you were pregnant. Congratulations, Kayla."

"Perhaps that's the one thing Meg didn't mention."

"No, she didn't. Have I said something to offend you?"

"No, but your gun did."

"Kayla, I am so sorry. I was in a weird space at that time and completely insane. There's no excuse for my behavior, which is why I came here with a piece offering."

"Okay, so tell me how I can make Mr. Wright great again?"

"You are so darn witty. I love it. Now, we both are aware that my wife is pregnant, correct?"

"Oh God!" Kayla said aloud.

"Yes, thank God. Those were my exact thoughts."

"Mr. Wright, I honestly don't know what to say."

"It was quite a surprise to me as well, Kayla. All my adult life I've felt inadequate. If a man can't produce, I felt that meant I was gay, which is how I got involved with Jared. Yes, Meg and I were on the verge of a divorce until she gave me this awesome news. I just knew it was a sign of redemption."

"It could be a sign of misfortune. With all due respect, you guys are at the age of an expected grandparent. I'm not trying to be rude or put a damper on your happiness, but how are you two going to raise a child after everything that has happened? How do you even know she's pregnant?"

"We got the ultrasound," he said, pulling out the pictures.

Although Kayla wasn't completely surprised by the photos, this new development was insane. The spawn of satan had convinced three men that they were fathers. It was clear to Kayla that Meg was acting out of desperation. She didn't have to do anything to get rid of Meg. Meg was literally destroying herself.

"Mr. Wright, why did you invite me here?"

"Oh, yes. I believe there comes a point in life where all should be forgiven as long as the attempt to reconcile is there. I would like to offer you and your husband exclusive memberships to all my clubs, three hundred thousand dollars cash, and ownership of two condominiums in Florida that rent at a thousand dollars weekly, which are occupied year-round. Does this offer sound appealing to you?"

"So do steak and mash potatoes until you serve it on top of a trash lid."

"I don't understand," he confusingly stated.

"What are your terms, Mr. Wright? What sewage are you asking me to crawl through before I reach this luxurious life style?"

"Oh…that's what you meant," he said and laughed, "Kayla, it's nothing like that. In exchange for this wonderful opportunity, all I ask is that you destroy anything incriminating that you have against my wife."

It was at that moment that Kayla realized that Meg finally thought she developed a scheme that would work. Dexter's cousin didn't seem to care about Meg's pregnancy, taking Dr. Roberts away was a fail, but getting her husband to think he was finally able to fertilize her eggs was the jackpot and the payoff was grand. Mr. Wright didn't appear to be a man with animalistic instincts, so Kayla could only assume that Meg didn't tell him the truth about all she had done.

"Mr. Wright-"

"Kayla, please. You've always called me Dylan," he interrupted.

"If you don't mind me asking, why did you shoot Meg?"

"Kayla, I would rather not discuss my personal affairs regarding my wife."

"I normally would respect that had you not shot at me."

"That's fair," he said, taking a deep breath. "Jared and I spent quite a bit of time together. He warned me that Meg was having an affair with a mutual colleague and was using my money for their personal escapades. Coincidentally, I was already suspicious of this person and when I confronted Meg, she said that he was your lover. Long story short, I assumed you were helping Meg with her affair."

"You were involved with Jared, so why would her affair make you so angry?"

"It was my money and you don't sleep with your husband's colleague. That's an entirely different level of disrespect. Anyway, I must admit that I was distraught by Jared's murder and I would be willing to pay anything to help catch the lowlife bastard that did it, but this child is my final chance to do something right in life."

Kayla almost felt sympathy for the old guy. He had no idea his wife killed his lover, which meant he had no idea about what evidence he wanted destroyed. She couldn't do it. Kayla knew she wasn't a saint, but she also refused to make a deal with the devil.

"Mr. Wright, I will consider your terms with one request of my own."

"I definitely feel as if I put a lot of thought into this proposal, but I'm willing to negotiate," he said, sounding stern.

"If Meg will agree to share what I have with you, then you can keep everything. You can keep the money, the membership, and everything else. I just want her out of my life for good."

"Wow, Kayla. Are you sure?"

"Yes," she responded, feeling a cloud of sorrow overcome her. She grabbed her purse and stood up from the chair. She knew that it was over for Meg. As she was about to exit the room, she turned around because she had to ask Dylan Wright one last question.

"Dylan, I know this is life changing for you, so you want to do what's right. Considering that you had questions about Meg's infidelity, what if the baby isn't yours?"

Dylan paused as if the thought never crossed his mind. There wasn't any way possible he could be that blind and oblivious to his wife's ways. He took another drink of champagne, walked up to Kayla, and looked her straight in the eyes.

"If this baby isn't mine, I will kill her myself."

Chapter 6

While Bryan waited for Kayla to arrive home, he started getting his work clothes together for the next day. He hadn't had the chance to tell Kayla that they were going to have to make immediate arrangements for Nicholas to go back to her mom's care, but it was understood that him staying with Bryan would only be temporary. Just as Bryan began unfolding an old pair of work dickies, one of Wayne's playboy pens fell from the pocket. Bryan sat down and reminisced about some of the wild times they had. Even though Wayne could be a pest at times, he was a day one homie. Although he obviously had to continue with his life, Bryan knew it wouldn't be the same without him.

Deep in thought, Bryan received a call from an unknown number. He answered, assuming it was a perspective client. Alex had already informed him that he would be handling the initial consultation for new business. He just didn't expect that business would start immediately.

"Hello, lover. It's always a pleasure to hear you speak," said the woman on the other end.

"You have got to be fucking kidding me right now. Why are you calling me, Jennie?"

"Bryan, that is no way to treat an old friend. Besides, we're practically family now that you have decided to stick your penis inside my niece."

"We will never be family, so you can erase that bullshit from your head."

"How about I just give you some head instead? It will be just like old times. I'll take you up to one of the cabins and we can get cozy and catch up on things. When are you free?"

"Jennie, you are mentally unstable, and you need counseling. Lose my number and forget that I ever existed, okay?"

"Bryan, I am sitting here babysitting your little angel as we speak. She's such a little doll and she has all her fingers and toes. I would think a man in your position would be a little nicer."

"Do you mean to tell me you are heartless enough to harm your own grandniece?"

"Bryan, how dare you insinuate such an appalling thing?"

"Jennie, what do you want from me? Shouldn't you be in prison for murdering your daughter and attempted murder of your son?"

"I am really getting offended by you labeling me as a monster, Bryan. Those are crude allegations and I don't appreciate you accusing me of such heinous crimes. Besides, my lawyers are Harvard graduates, so justice prevailed. Perhaps you should line you up a lawyer team. My niece surely intends on taking every dime that you get."

"Jennie, you need to get a life and stay out of mine. There are plenty of under age boys that would love for you to stalk them."

"Have you considered the fact that I am the most powerful woman you will ever meet? You should watch what you say to me."

"You are a psychotic stalker and I regret that I ever met you."

"I would think you would know how to speak to me after Wayne's unfortunate accident."

"Jennie, if you ever in your fuckin' life threaten-"

Jennie Jenson hung up before Bryan could finish his response. Sleeping with a married woman was the worst mistake he had ever made in his life. This woman was Bryan's living nightmare. Threatening him was one thing, but involving a child was an entirely different level of deviousness. Talking with her only enhanced his aggravation. From what Renee said, Bryan was under the impression that Jon Junior was involved with Wayne's death. Now, he wasn't sure if Jennie was trying to get him riled up or she put the hit out on Wayne. Then again, maybe Jennie pulled the trigger herself. She did have a fling with Wayne before she got arrested. It was like walking through a maze and Bryan's head was spinning. He had to talk to his mom and get some answers. He planned on leaving as soon as Kayla walked through the door.

Kayla arrived about 15 minutes later still perplexed about her meetings with Mr. Wright. She checked the mailbox, noticing that Bryan had received a letter from the judicial court system. This could only mean one thing. Jennie's niece was probably filing for child support since Bryan had been procrastinating about taking the paternity test.

"You have an urgent letter," Kayla said, without saying hello.

Bryan could hear the negativity in her tone and didn't respond as he opened the letter. He had too much going on to argue and didn't want to say anything that he would regret. Just as Kayla had suspected, the judge had petitioned an order for child support based on the results of a paternity test. Bryan threw the papers on the table, went upstairs, and slammed the bedroom door. Kayla was exhausted from the earlier events that had already taken place, so she didn't bother following Bryan. Instead, she went into Nicholas's room and saw him happily playing with his Lego toys. She was thankful that Nicholas seemed oblivious to the chaotic circumstances surrounding her and Bryan. She was also excited that he would have someone to play with soon.

"Hey baby boy, what'cha doing?"

"Momma, I'm not a baby any more. I am a growing young man."

"I know that, Sweetie, but you'll always be mommy's baby boy no matter what."

"I know that momma, but I have to protect my family and become the man of the house in case something happens to you or daddy."

"You don't have to worry about anything happening to mommy or daddy anytime soon, Sweetie. I will say that I think it is very commendable of you to want to protect us and your baby brother or sister."

"Grandma said it's going to be a girl. She said it was a lot of bad people in this world and I would have to protect my little sister from the predators."

"When did you go see grandma?"

"I stayed over Grandma Irene's house today when daddy went to work. Daddy must have had a bad day at work. When we got home, he was very upset. He told the lady to stop fucking calling him."

"Nicholas, you know better than to repeat what grown ups say when they use bad words."

"I'm sorry, momma. I just never heard daddy that upset before."

"It's okay, son. Everyone has bad days sometimes. Plus, your dad has been under a lot of stress lately, so he's trying to pick up where he left off."

"Were the people who shot daddy the bad people that grandma was talking about?"

"No, Baby. Daddy's situation was an accident, which is why I always tell you never to play with weapons."

"Someone should have told the person who shot daddy that."

"You are right, son. Just be mindful of what you repeat, okay? Go ahead and get washed up for dinner."

"Okay, momma. I love you."

"I love you too, Baby."

Kayla closed his door not knowing what to think. Why would Bryan's mom tell her son that predators were after her unborn baby? Had she lost her damn mind and who was this mystery woman calling Bryan that he failed to mention? Perhaps Bryan and this mystery woman was the reason Wayne got shot. What Nicholas said didn't come across like Bryan was cheating, but he was hiding something. Kayla had enough of the secrets. She decided it was time for Bryan to come clean about his secrets and for her to tell him everything about Meg, which meant showing him the video.

Chapter 7

After getting Nicholas settled and in the bed, it was time for Kayla to call it a night. Bryan was still up eating popcorn by the time she had finished showering. Although the television was on, she could tell he wasn't really watching it.

"Nicholas seems to think you went back to work today."

"His assumption was accurate. I was going to tell you that my release papers came through and Alex needs me back immediately."

"Are you able to do all that heavy lifting and constant walking so soon?" She asked.

"I probably won't be able to do everything I was doing beforehand, but Alex understands that. We have a few more new contracts, so he hired a few extra workers."

"Are you going to go take the paternity test tomorrow?"

"No, I have about three weeks to get that handled. I'm going to take care of business first," responded Bryan, muddled by the question.

"I understand that, but the paternity business affects your work business, which affects our personal business."

"Look Kayla, I'm going to handle things on my own time, okay?"

"Well, while you're on your own time, could you also tell your mother to stop telling my son that predators are after our baby?"

"Alright, Kayla, whatever you say," said Bryan, not having a clue what she was talking about.

"Did Nicholas tell you what she told him?"

"No, he did not. As a matter of fact, I'm about to go and holla at momma in a minute."

"Bryan, are you seriously going to go over there this late?"

"What do you mean? My momma doesn't have a curfew and neither do I."

"Okay, Mr. Smartass, just make sure you're not trying to meet up with the bitch that you told to fuck off earlier in front of my son."

Bryan looked at his wife and took a deep breath. The old him would have launched a full-fledged argument. He didn't want that type of marriage. If things were going to change, he knew he needed to be an example of that change.

"Baby, I wasn't aware that Nicholas was listening. Renee had call about some BS, so I reacted and I'm sorry."

Bryan hated to lie, but he knew he couldn't tell Kayla the truth about Jennie calling him. She seemed to be under enough stress at work, so he didn't want to add anything extra. He remembered his mom being traumatized from the miscarriages she had, so he didn't want that to happen to Kayla.

"What did Renee want?"

"She was still upset about you and her going at each other in the hospital. She said that she feels you should have called her and apologized. I told her it was a delicate moment for everyone, so she needed to get over it."

"Oh, well, I'm sorry, too. My emotions and hormones are all over the place and I can't help it," Kayla admitted as she began to cry.

"It's okay, baby, we're in this together."

"Maybe I should call her and apologize. I would lose my mind if I lost you, so I could only imagine the hurt she is going through from losing her child and her husband."

"Baby, don't worry about that nonsense. What happened to my cousin was a long time ago. You don't have to apologize to her for taking the anger she has for me out on you. I wouldn't dare allow you to apologize for something that she is festering from before I met you."

"Are you sure? I know that she doesn't have it in her heart to apologize, so I don't mind being the bigger person."

"Kayla, I got this. I don't want you to worry about anything. I need you to focus on your health and well being for you and the baby. We need our baby coming out with all ten fingers and toes," he joked, trying to lighten the mood.

Bryan knew he had to do everything in his power to prevent her from calling Renee. He quickly saw how even a little protective lie could get out of hand. Although he wanted to tell the truth, he just didn't feel the need to bring up Jennie at that time.

"As a matter of fact, I'm going to wait and talk to my mom in the morning. I want to know what's on your mind. How have you been feeling lately?"

"I guess I've been feeling okay outside of the normal morning sickness and mild cravings. I don't remember being as sick with Nicholas, but I know every pregnancy is different."

"Are you craving something now? I can go and get you something if you would like."

"No, silly. I'm fine."

"Is there anything else you want to talk about or something that's going on at work that you wanna tell me?"

Kayla knew that this was her opportunity to come clean about everything. It was time to allow Bryan into her other world by showing him the gruesome video of Meg that she witnessed in person. She also wanted to tell him about Dylan's offer and their opportunity to be set for life. She wanted him to help her sort out all the chaos that Meg had created in her life.

As she slowly retrieved her phone from the table, she thought about Bryan's reaction. She knew he would demand her to immediately quit her job and he would probably turn in the video himself, fearing for her safety. Realistically, she couldn't expect Bryan to be okay with this. Kayla wasn't ready for the aftermath that could result from Bryan forcing her to turn the video in to the police. Surely, Dylan would think that she betrayed him and apparently, this man was capable of anything. He suggested killing his own wife if he was deceived by the paternity results, so he was more than capable of killing both her and Bryan.

"Uh...no, babe. Everything is fine. I'm just going to play a few games on my phone and rest."

"Are you sure?"

"Yes babe. I'm sure. These are just normal hormonal issues that some women must unfortunately deal with during pregnancy... There's nothing for you to be worried about."

The next morning, Kayla's mood swings had transitioned to her feeling nauseated. She ran to the bathroom and threw up several times before she was able to compose herself. With all the madness going on, she had forgot to tell Bryan that Dr. Roberts had rescheduled her ultrasound for today since today would be the last official day that she would report to him. Since Bryan had suddenly went back to work, Kayla knew the chances of him being able to make it to the appointment would be slim, but she planned on calling him once she got ready to leave the house.

Kayla went to wake Nicholas, but much to her surprise, Bryan had left a note saying he loved her and that he was going to drop off Nicholas. She clearly had to have been in a deep sleep, because she didn't hear them getting ready or leaving this morning. She was that much more grateful, knowing she had such a thoughtful husband.

After putting on her work clothes, she went down to the kitchen and grabbed a Sprite to help with her morning sickness. She ate a few saltine crackers, but she knew that wasn't going to be enough to satisfy her hunger. She had a craving for a bacon egg sandwich, but she didn't feel like cooking anything. She figured she'd grab a breakfast bar and stop by McDonalds on her way to work.

———

Kayla grabbed her purse and took another sip of Sprite before getting ready to head out of the door. She had almost spilled her drink on the floor from being startled by the doorbell. Kayla couldn't imagine who could be visiting that early in the morning, so she wasn't going to answer without Bryan being there. The garage was closed, so it was a wonder at how anyone would even know she was there. She quietly tiptoed to the front door and looked out the peephole.

"You have got to be fucking kidding me," she whispered to herself.

Chapter 8

Kayla stood there looking out of the peephole as she attempted to register what was happening at her front door. She didn't want to believe her own eyesight, but there was no denying of what was happening. It was no secret as to how this stranger got a hold to her address. The bigger question was why was she there? The woman that stood there with a child on her hip was a splitting image of Jennie's deceased daughter Erica. She was about the same height, had the same light-skinned complexion, and slim figure as Erica. Their resemblance was so eerie that it was almost like looking at Erica's ghost. There was no mystery about who this woman was standing at her doorstep. It could be none other than Jackie Jenson, Jennie Jenson's niece.

Kayla was still trying to fathom the fact that this lady had the balls to come to her house, unannounced, and have a baby with her that wasn't yet proven to be Bryan's child. It was apparent to her that Jackie had to be just as mentally challenged as her goofy aunt. If it wasn't for the baby being in her arms, Kayla would have introduced herself with her stainless steel by her side.

After about 20 seconds, Kayla felt herself about to vomit again. She quickly went back upstairs to the bathroom and had to lie down after her episode. She thought she heard a few people outside having a conversation, but the voices were so faint that she couldn't really tell. Either way, she didn't have the energy to get up from her bed at that particular time to investigate. Little did Kayla know, the Universe was working in her favor. She had no idea that Jennie Jenson was also standing out front to Jackie's side, out of her peephole's view.

After about 15 minutes, Kayla got up to retrieve the nausea medication that her doctor had given her. She only took it as a last resort, but she knew she probably wouldn't make it through the day without it. It had been about 10 minutes since the chiming of the doorbell had faded and the muffled voices that she had heard had ceased. Kayla assumed that her unwanted guest had left, and she was happy that she avoided the confrontation. She wasn't sure what she would have said or how she would've reacted to anything that Jackie felt the need to discuss without proof of paternity. She wondered what driving force caused Jackie to show up at their home after all this time. Had Bryan had a conversation with Jackie and hadn't told her about it?

After finishing up in the house, Kayla got in her car and opened the garage. As she was pulling out, she saw her neighbor standing across the street at the end of her own yard as if she was waiting on the mailman. Kayla was aware that he didn't run that early, so it must have been something else that had her neighbor out there. Ms. Rose was a retired homemaker in her late 60's, so she kept a good eye out on the neighborhood. Kayla drove to the end of her driveway and got out of the car.

"Good morning Ms. Rose. How are you?"

"Hello, Dear. You are certainly glowing this morning."

"Thank you. I've been having a bad case of morning sickness today."

"Oh, I'm sorry to hear that, Hun. What'cha need to do is get'cha some ginger, honey, and mint juice. That'll take it all away."

"Yes ma'am. What brings you out here so early?" Kayla asked.

"Well, I was sittin' on my porch and I saw you had visitors. Now, I mind my business until I saw one of them gals peekin' in ya front window."

Kayla was confused. What did she mean by 'one of those gals' in her window? She couldn't have been referring to the baby. Kayla decided to pretend as if she didn't see anyone.

"Well, Bryan said he told one of his associates to come by and see what type of treatment we needed for our flower bushes."

"Nah. These gals didn't look like no gardeners. One of'em had a baby on her hip."

"Oh, there were two women?"

"Yes indeed. Now, the one with the baby stood there watching the other. I walked my tail on' round there and told them that y'all weren't home and I would send the picture I took of them to let y'all know they came by."

"Do you still have the picture?"

"Baby, I don't have no picture. I said that to scare'em off," she admitted and laughed.

Kayla pretended to be amused with her, but she knew that this was no laughing matter. After saying goodbye to Ms. Rose, she thought about what was witnessed. Why did this chick bring someone else with her and why would this someone move out of view and try to peek through her window? Did Jackie hire an attorney to serve Bryan with more papers? Kayla was that much more fed up that Bryan hadn't taken care of his business. She was going to call him immediately and give him a piece of her mind.

"Hello, beautiful. Did you get some rest?" Bryan asked.

"Yes, I did until my morning was disturbed by your alleged baby momma with her side kick showing up to our house."

"You've got to be kidding me right now. Jennie and Jackie showed up to our house?"

Kayla was startled. What would make Bryan assume it was Jennie that Jackie was with? Kayla recalled the conversation about Bryan telling someone to leave him the fuck alone. It all started to come together. The woman that Bryan went off on wasn't Renee. It had to be Jennie or Jackie. Bryan lied right to her face.

"The woman you hung up on was Jennie Jensen, wasn't it? You lied to me!" Kayla yelled.

"Listen baby. I did not want to upset you and the baby, so yes, I lied. But-"

"I can not believe you, Bryan! How could you lie right to my face?"

"Baby, I didn't think it was that big of a deal."

"You didn't think that the woman who killed her own husband, attempted to kill her son, and caused havoc in our relationship wouldn't be something that you should mention?"

"Kayla, you're acting as if you caught me screwing this woman or something. What happened yesterday was no big deal."

"It was big enough for you to lie to me about it."

"Okay, listen to me. Jennie called me out of the blue and said that I need to step up and be a father to her niece's child. She made some threats about child support and her niece taking me to court. I told her to mind her damn business and to stop fuckin' calling me. That was it."

"If it was that innocent then how come you couldn't just tell me? Why would you have me thinking I should call Renee and apologize to her?"

"Why would I want to make Jennie relevant in any type of way in our marriage? I frankly don't understand why you're not able to comprehend and respect that," Bryan argued.

"That's the reason why you didn't want me to call Renee last night. She would have busted your ass out in front of me."

"If the shoe was on the other foot, I would..."

Kayla hung up without allowing him to finish his statement or any other sorry excuse that he had. They were supposed to be a team and him lying about this situation only made her more suspicious of everything else that had happened in the last few months. Who really shot Bryan and why? Maybe he was still creeping around with Jennie and she shot both him and Wayne. All Kayla knew was that she had enough on her plate dealing with Meg, so the last thing she needed was an extra serving of Jennie Jenson.

Chapter 9

Bryan wanted to call his wife back, but he could only step outside for so long. He had already explained to his work team that his wife was pregnant, so they expected the occasional walkouts. He couldn't believe after all this time these women would have the nerve to show up to his home. What disturbed him even more was that Jennie had the nerve to step her ass on his property. He knew the she was the real mastermind of it all. What were they planning to do? Did they have intentions to scare or jump on his pregnant wife? That was the last straw for Bryan. He knew he had to call in a favor.

"Hey Floyd, man, I need you to do me a solid." Bryan Proposed to his cousin.

"You know I got'cha. What do you need, B?"

"Man, I need you to come grab my license, registration, my truck, and do this paternity gig for me, man."

"Man, stop playing, B. What's good, though?"

"I'm dead serious. I'm almost ninety-nine percent sure it's not my baby, but I need to be one hundred percent sure."

"Are you for real? Man, you don't want to know if the little shorty is yours?"

"It's deeper than that, man. If this baby is mine this other psycho woman I dealt with is going to put the baby through hell because I slept with her niece."

"She can't be crazy enough to hurt her own flesh and blood."

"Cuz, this bitch pistol whipped her own son and cut her daughter's brakes."

"Damn, what type of crazy bitches are you dealin' with, man?"

"That's just my haunted past catching up with me, but I really need this done like today."

"Alright. I don't fully agree with it, but I guess you have no choice. I'm not with having any kids n' shit hurt or tortured."

"I appreciate it and you know I got all of your expenses covered along with a little extra."

"It's all good. This is what we do. We cover each other by any means."

After hanging up with him, Bryan knew that Floyd's last statement meant that he was going to owe him big time. At that moment, it didn't matter. This was what had to be done. Bryan knew that the test facilitators wouldn't be able to physically distinguish the difference between him and Floyd. To make everything even sweeter, no member of the Jenson family and Bryan were allowed in the facility at the same time due to the prior court proceedings that had taken place involving the death of Jimmie Jenson and his daughter. As a matter of fact, Jennie wasn't supposed to contact Bryan under any circumstances. Jennie obviously didn't care about the laws, which made Bryan certain that he was doing the right thing. He felt as if he was not only protecting his wife and unborn child, but Jackie's baby as well.

Meanwhile, on the other side of town, Kayla had finally made it to her office. Dexter hadn't shown up yet for their usual "tea" discussion, but she didn't really mind since she was still trying to decipher the events from this morning. If Jennie Jenson was outside of their home, she was definitely in violation of her court order. Furthermore, Jackie is a grown ass woman with means to communicate with Bryan on her own.

It was clear to Kayla that the women came to her home to start trouble. It was even more shameful that they used a poor, defenseless baby in attempt to lower Kayla's guard. Now that Kayla knew that Jackie was just as messy as her aunt, she was going to make sure that hot lead was loaded for anyone threatening her or her family on her property. The sad part of it all was that Kayla wanted nothing more than to have a normal life and raise her growing family. Everything that was going on around her was chaotic and Kayla knew that something had to give soon.

Kayla's final appointment with Dr. Roberts to have her ultrasound done was about an hour away. Finding out the sex of her child was a huge moment for her and she wanted someone to go with her. Bryan obviously couldn't make it and she was pissed off at his lying ass anyway. She didn't want Ms. Irene's negative vibes around her and her mother had Nicholas. The only other person she was willing to consider was Dexter. Kayla and Dexter's supervisor had a great work relationship, so she knew it would be okay if she took him with her down to the laboratory. She locked her office door and headed towards Dexter's hall.

"Hey, Jamie. How are you, Sweetie? Have you seen Dexter today?" Kayla asked, rounding the corner.

"Hey, Hun. Actually, I haven't seen him all morning. I thought he might be running a few errands for you. Let me see if he called out today," Jamie said as she leaned over to check the attendance log.

"That's certainly unusual. I don't think I've ever known Dexter to call out, but there's a first for everything," Kayla joked.

"I know, right. Dexter is the only person on my team that I can depend on through rain, sleet, and snow."

"I second that emotion," Kayla agreed.

"No, he hasn't called out today. Uhm...perhaps he took an early lunch and forgot to tell me, or I forgot to write it down."

"Oh, that's fine. I'll just check back later. If he comes in within the next forty-five minutes, could you let him know I'm looking for him?"

"Sure thing, Kayla."

Kayla left the area feeling strange about Dexter's abstinence. It was safe to accuse Dexter of a lot of things like being nosy and gossiping, but never for being tardy. She decided not to get herself worked up by allowing negative thoughts of something bad happening to entertain her mind. Dexter probably overslept and would call her soon, laughing about what happened the night before that caused him to oversleep.

Arriving at her appointment, Kayla knew that being around Dr. Roberts would be awkward. They normally chatted about life and lightly gossiped about coworkers in the hospital, but soon enough, Dr. Roberts would probably be the main talk of the hospital. His wild parties were one thing, but getting a married woman, who was a top administrator of the hospital, pregnant was unthinkable. Did he not care about getting fired if the secret got out? Better yet, where was Dr. Roberts going to hide if Dylan Wright discovered he was raw-dogging his wife? Sadly, Dr. Roberts was clueless about the cold-blooded killers he was dealing with.

"I'm sure your son will be happy," Dr. Roberts said, breaking into Kayla's thoughts.

"I'm sorry Dr. Roberts. My mind was in another world. What did you say?"

"Oh, that's okay. It happens to me all the time. I said congratulations. You will be welcoming a baby girl soon and I'm sure your son will be happy."

Kayla's mood instantly changed. Deep down inside she wanted a girl, but convinced herself it would be another boy, so she wouldn't be disappointed. Kayla's excitement about her reveal had surpassed everything she had been through that morning. She was finally having a mini her. She couldn't wait to get back to her floor and tell everyone the good news.

"Hey, Kayla," Jamie said, almost out of breath.

"Oh hi, Jamie. Did you catch up with Dexter? I have something exciting to tell him."

"That's kind of why I've been running around to find you."

"Oh, I'm sorry. I had an appointment with Dr. Roberts."

"Kayla, I just received a call from Dexter's mom. They found his phone and keys outside on the ground beside his car."

"Where is he?"

"That's the thing. No one has seen or heard from him since last night. His mother said he never leaves without his phone, so she knows its foul play. The police told her that she has to wait twenty-four hours to file a missing persons report."

Kayla didn't know what to say. She had just spoken with Dexter yesterday. How could he be missing today? An intense feeling of anxiety had overcome her as she stepped back to sit in the first chair she saw. It seems as if everything was moving in slow motion and she could see Jamie's lips moving but couldn't comprehend what she was saying. The last thing that Kayla remembered seeing before almost passing out was a text message from Meg that read: *How is Dexter?*

Kayla quickly pulled herself together and walked towards the door where she saw Meg exiting. *Her evil ass couldn't have gotten that far*, thought Kayla as she visually scanned the parking lot. Kayla hoped she'd be able to maintain her composure since they both were pregnant. She also considered the possibility that this was a scheme created by Meg in order to make her have a miscarriage. It didn't take working in the medical field to know that any physical altercation could harm a pregnancy. Furthermore, Kayla didn't feel that Meg actually wanted a baby. She felt that Meg only got pregnant because she assumed it would help keep her out of prison.

"Are you looking for me?" Meg asked, smoking a cigarette next to a bench in the far left corner of the building.

"Are you seriously smoking a cigarette right now? You are too old to be smoking while you're pregnant. This is just one more of the many reasons that you should be the last person to conceive."

"Shut the hell up, Kayla, damn. You didn't screw me to have this child, so why are you worried about what happens to me or it?"

"Meg, you don't even know who screwed you to have your child."

"Your little clap backs are so cute and funny. Too bad your little sidekick isn't here laughing with you, now is it?"

"If I find out that you had anything to do with Dexter's disappearance, your ass will be featured on the real orange and black. You are not above justice."

"You must be living in a dream world. Dylan won't allow that to happen. He is very ecstatic about having this baby. You should have seen the look on his face when I told him he was going to be a father."

"Do you think he would be just as ecstatic if he knew there were ten other possible baby daddies?"

"Oh my gosh! You are so freaking funny, Kayla. You should have tried comedy instead of nursing."

"And you should try Jesus instead of murder."

"You're joking, right? Do you really think out of all the bullshit you've done that your little ass is somehow holy all of a sudden, Kayla? You need the Holy Spirit more than me."

"Do you have a video of me slicing someone's throat? Am I the one running around telling three different men that they are daddies? I don't think so."

"So that's what this is all about. You think that you can still blackmail me by threatening me with that video." Meg said.

"I never blackmailed you about anything. You did the dirty work yourself. I simply asked you to stay the hell away from me but you did the opposite. I could have turned your wicked ass into the cops a long time ago if I wanted to."

"Kayla, if there's one thing in life that I want you to remember is this. I'm in control. I will dictate everything that happens from this point forward."

"Meg, you need serious help and I sincerely pray for that unborn child."

"Hey, don't you worry about me. My life is grand. Dylan and I are going to be great parents. We intend on moving out of the country and allowing our first born to experience the entire world."

"Okay, so how is the real baby's father going to feel about taking his baby out of the country? Or is he already dead?"

Meg gave Kayla a cold stare and instantly dropped her cigarette. She looked up towards the sky, closed her eyes, and blew out her remaining cigarette smoke. Kayla braced herself just in case Meg decided to do something crazy. She walked up to Kayla, placed her hand on Kayla's shoulder, and got close to her ear.

"As you ask your Jesus to forgive me for my sins, also ask Him to forgive Jared and Dexter for their sins. They will need forgiveness much sooner than me," she said as she walked away toward the parking lot.

Kayla hurried over to a grassy area and vomited. She didn't have to assume what Meg was saying by putting Jared and Dexter in the same category. Meg and Dexter hated one another from the start but that was no reason to do whatever she did or had someone to do to him. Meg must have found out that Dexter's new lover was one of her alleged baby's daddy's cousins. She probably thought Dexter would run his mouth to the hospital staff about the affair and it would get back to Dylan. Meg was relentless and willing to do anything to have things her way. Kayla couldn't even go back inside of the hospital. Instead, she went to her car and cried tears like a baby.

Kayla thought about all the laughs that she shared with Dexter. No matter what type of day she was having, Dexter was there to save it. Even though he told everyone else's business, she couldn't recall a time that he had told anything she asked him to keep in secrecy. He was the closest thing she had to a best friend. She almost didn't want to be there at all, knowing he was missing.

The more Kayla thought about it, the angrier she became. She knew that if she continued to allow this woman to cross the line that Meg may end up hurting her too or worse. Meg was extremely calculated, so more than likely, she would continue to go after the people that Kayla cared about and love the most. It was time for Kayla to make a decision that would change the course of everyone's life. She reached in her pocket and retrieved her phone. She pulled up the necessary contact and created a message that read: *Say hello and goodbye to Meg's true baby daddy.* She took a deep breath and sent the video of Meg murdering Jared to Dylan.

Chapter 10

Bryan was finishing up the outdoor measurements with his crew members as his workday was coming to an end. He had a lot on his mind as he tried to focus on the business plans for the new clients. He couldn't put his finger on it, but something wasn't adding up between Wayne's death, Jessie's strange pop-up, and Alex acting weird. Even though Jennie mentioned Wayne's death as a threat tactic, she couldn't have done it since she just got released. Wayne's death was a few months ago and him knowing Jennie, her twisted ass would have called and bragged about it then. Bryan was beginning to feel overwhelmed by the mystery of it all.

"Hey, Bryan. Can I have a word with you real quick?" Alex asked, stepping away from the other crew members.

"What's going on, man?" Bryan responded, wiping sweat from his forehead.

"Here's the deal, man." He began, lowering his voice. "Jesse has been coming to my office with some wild accusations about you and your family."

"You're kidding, right? What type of accusations?"

"They sounded so off the wall that I wasn't going to even mention it until an officer came by the office earlier. He asked me a few general questions about her and then asked was I aware of her disappearance."

"What? Man, that crazy girl ain't missing. If anything, she's missing her damn brain. What did she tell you about me?"

"Okay, Jesse came by my office the other day claiming that Wayne once told her that your family was connected to the mob. She also said that she thought you all were out to kill her because of you getting shot and that she felt as if she was being followed. I personally thought it was ridiculous and that she wanted some attention since Wayne was gone. However, the police came by and said that Jesse's family filed a missing person report on her."

"Man, this is the first time I've heard of this bizarre mess. I'm the one that got shot. The police should be investigating her ass!" Bryan exclaimed.

"I know, man. It's all odd. You wouldn't have happened to have seen or talked to her lately, have you?"

"I honestly wouldn't have a reason to."

"Oh…okay. I just wanted to give you a heads up in case the police come back and I'm not here."

"Alright, Alex, I definitely got it handled and I appreciate the heads up."

After walking off from Alex, something felt even stranger. Alex said that the police questioned him earlier while he was still at the office. If the police had questions for Bryan, why wouldn't Alex just have directed them to the job site where Bryan had been all day? Furthermore, when did Jesse have all this time to tell Alex about her personal discussions with Wayne? It was funny that Jesse would go missing the day after she had a conversation with Alex instead of directly after Wayne's death. Although Bryan still had intentions to speak with his mom about Jon Junior, it sounded like boss man, Alex had a separate situation with Jesse. Alex must have assumed that Bryan would be an easy target to blame Jesse's disappearance on since Alex knew that they had bad history. Luckily for Bryan, he was not oblivious to whatever scheme that Alex might have conjured in his mind.

About an hour later, Bryan left work and went directly to his mom's house. He needed understanding at this point. He was already in debt with Floyd regarding the paternity test, so he needed to know what extra debt was created with Jon Junior without his knowledge. Bryan knew that his mom was going to put up a fight and try not to give him information for his protection, but it wasn't going to work today. Without Nicholas being around, he had the opportunity to push Ms. Irene to her limits if he had to.

"Momma, I'm here," yelled Bryan, opening the front door.

"Boy, why are you yelling in this small, enclosed space?" Ms. Irene asked as she continued washing dishes.

"I'm sorry, Ma. I'm just making sure you're here, that's all."

"Where am I gonna go, son?"

"I don't know. You may have had a hot date or something," he joked.

"Boy, if you don't stop, you can turn right back around and head on out that door."

"I'm just playing with you momma, dang."

"What do you want, son?"

"What? I can't come by to see the love of my life?"

"Your wife is at home where you should be."

"Okay, momma, whatever you say, but I do have something that I need to talk to you about."

"I have things I need to do, son, so keep it brief."

It became apparent to Bryan that his mother was getting agitated. Either she could sense where he was going with the conversation or she had already talked to Renee. For him, this was the perfect time to put everything out on the table.

"I had a talk with Renee the other day," he began, waiting for her reaction.

"And?"

"And she seems to think that I need to discuss Jon Junior with you."

"I don't know why she feels the need to open her damn mouth. She needs to worry about her own damn business and stop asking me for money to send that dead beat."

"Yeah, I'm sure you're right, but I need to know about this deal with Jon Junior."

"What deal with Jon Junior?"

"Momma, I have a lot going on and I am on a need to know basis. What happened at the hospital? Why were you speaking French?"

Ms. Irene glanced at him and quickly turned her head. Walking away from the sink, she dried her hands and continued twisting them together as she sat down.

"It's okay, momma. I can handle anything. Just tell me what happened."

"Son, we all fall short sometimes. Let's pray that our Father is understanding and that the generational curse is broken."

"Momma, how are you going to break a generational curse when you're telling our son that demons are after his unborn sibling?"

"Did you come here to argue? Cause if you did, I don't have time."

"I came here to find out why Jon Junior thinks I owe him."

"Son, just go home and take care of your family."

"Momma, stop avoiding the question and answer me."

"Son, please go home...go home...go home."

"I'm not leaving this house until you...tell...me…what Jon Junior has on me," yelled Bryan, slamming his fist on the table.

"HE ENDED WAYNE!" She yelled back.

There was a moment of silence. Ms. Irene had finally confirmed Bryan's initial thoughts. His family not only killed an innocent man, but his best man.

"Why, momma? Why couldn't y'all just wait and talk to me. I wasn't dead yet. That was my best friend, momma."

"Son, I know what you may think. I'm sorry things had to go down that way, but Wayne's intentions weren't good in the end."

"Momma, why are you talking to me as if I'm a kid and you just put down my dog? This is my life, momma. I got kids and a wife to protect, so I need answers."

Irene took a deep breath. "Back in the day, Wayne's mom, Gloria Dean, and I worked the streets together. My ranking was better than hers and she didn't like it, but we stayed cordial because we had to do what we had to do. Long story short, I was beat up pretty badly by a customer and I lost the baby that I was carrying."

"Damn, momma, I'm sorry. I wasn't trying to make you relive those painful memories."

"It's okay, son. You wanted the truth. A few weeks later, the boss man and I found out that Wayne's mother had arranged for the man to have me raped and killed and to have it staged like it was a robbery gone wrong. The only reason he didn't get the chance to carry out the plan was because the gun jammed, and he was scared off by someone banging at the door. Boss man later found that same man and he confessed everything before losing his life. As a punishment for her disloyalty, I was ordered to shoot Gloria Dean."

"Wayne said his daddy told him his mother left them."

"I said I shot her. I didn't say I killed her."

"Okay, so, where is she?"

"She disappeared, and no one knew of her whereabouts until..." Ms. Irene paused and put her head down.

"Until what, momma?"

"Your Uncle, Jon Senior had received a call from one of our old acquaintances. He said that Gloria Dean was on her death bed talking out the side of her head. In one of her confessions, she admitted that she had been reaching out to her estranged son for some time and she blamed me for her having to abandon him. She told him I ruined their lives and that the best revenge would be for him to take you from me."

"And you actually think that Wayne listened to a woman he hadn't heard from for practically his entire life and attempted to carry out her wishes?"

"It wasn't a wish, son. It was an order. Her final order before she died."

"I do not believe that, momma. Do you know how crazy that sounds? This guy has been my ace for years, so why wouldn't you tell me about all this a long time ago?"

"Son, no one knew Gloria Dean even had a son until she wrote the letter on her death bed. Wayne wasn't going to stop until the order was completed."

"I still can't believe this, momma. All that carrying out orders mess is behind us now. We have a new life, remember? All of this sounds too convenient. Besides, Wayne wasn't a part of that life. He wasn't even the one with the gun in the first place. Jesse had the gun. This is a faulty scenario created by my family in attempt to justify murdering my friend. Y'all couldn't just leave the past alone, could you?"

"Okay, son. I'm done with it."

———

"Furthermore, how can y'all be sure that Wayne even got the letter from his mother?"

"Son, some things aren't what they seem. Family sometimes doesn't act like family and friends are your worst enemies."

"No shit, momma!"

"Boy, I will knock the teeth outta yo mouth if you ever speak to me that way again!"

"Momma, I'm sorry. I'm speaking out of anger right now but look at what you're telling me. My best friend was murdered by my cousin because my mom shot his mom who wanted revenge from her death bed. This ain't no damn circus, so stop mistaking me for a clown!"

"Bryan, you don't know everything, so just shut up."

"No, Irene. I'm not believing some made-up revenge theory to justify shooting my best friend," Bryan argued, walking towards the door.

"Wayne wasn't your best friend, son. I know that he got the letter because your dad told me. Your dad is Wayne's father, too."

Chapter 11

Kayla sat in her car and theorized how Dylan would react to the video. Exposing his wife for killing his lover was risky and the outcome wasn't going to benefit anyone. Even if Dylan went into a rage and hurt Meg, he could still blame Kayla for ruining their lives by exposing the truth to him. Even years from now there was a possibility of him reminiscing and seeking revenge. Kayla began to second guess her decision, but it was too late. She waited in the parking lot well over 30 minutes to see if Dylan was going to respond. Once she felt confident that he wasn't, she headed home. *Perhaps his phone was off, and he didn't get it*, she thought. Regardless of her moment of optimism, deep down Kayla knew that every minute she was waiting was probably the exact number of times Dylan had watched the video.

Once Kayla arrived home, she instantly noticed Bryan's truck wasn't in the garage. With all the chaos going on, she didn't even think about the fact that Nicholas was now with her mother. She called Bryan to see if he was off work, but he didn't answer. Being that it was his first day back on the job, she figured he may be working late. Even though they argued earlier, she really could use the distraction and comfort of her husband.

Kayla came up with a spontaneous idea. She decided she would pop up and surprise Bryan with the sex of their baby. She wasn't sure about his new location, so she grabbed her phone to call Alex. She waited for the phone to ring, but there was complete silence. She looked at her phone to make sure she hit dial, but her phone indicated that she was talking. Just as she was about to hang up and redial, she heard talking. She said hello, but no one said anything. She turned up the volume to see if she could understand what was being said.

"You'd better make damn sure that this is the last time that I get your little stupid ass out of trouble, boy. What in the hell were you thinking?" A man with a raspy voice screamed.

Kayla couldn't for the life of her recognize the voice. She looked at her phone again and noticed that the number she called was saved as Alex. She assumed that Alex's number had changed, and she probably just had the old number. The men continued to argue, and Kayla was about to hang up until she heard the man say Alex's name.

"Dad, I'm only saying that there had to be another way. What if that was my child?"

"That could have been anyone's child from Mount Everest to the Sahara Desert. Are you kidding me right now, Knucklehead? Beyond that, a man of your position is not supposed to degrade himself by impregnating a whore."

"Who are we to place judgment, dad? Maybe Jesse was just misunderstood."

"Oh, yeah? Wasn't she the one living with your employee that was murdered not too long ago? She had to have known you were married. Did she desperately fall into your arms while you were stroking her hair in front of the boy's casket?"

"Are you seriously making jokes about someone's dead son? The things that you're saying sound stupid and don't matter."

"I ought to come over there and rip off one of your ears, boy. I guess it didn't matter that she threatened your life and your marriage either, huh? I guess it also doesn't matter that she threatened to ruin your reputation, your job, and our family business, huh?"

"I guess you just solved all of the above, dad. Now, if you'll excuse me, I have to call my wife. Wait a minute. This is weird. My phone says I've been talking to someone for five minutes. Hello...Hello? This is so weird," Alex said, very puzzled.

"Is someone on the phone? Were they listening? What did they hear?" His dad continued to question from the background.

"Dad calm down. It was probably a pocket dial or something."

Kayla didn't know what to do. She knew that Alex would probably observe his phone and notice it was an incoming call opposed to a pocket dial. She wasn't sure if Alex had her number saved as a contact or not. All she knew was that she couldn't hang up at this point. Alex would know that the person on the line probably heard everything. She kept the phone on mute and waited to see what he would do. He ended the call and called Kayla's number back to back several times.

Back at Ms. Irene's home, the air was so tense that even a sword couldn't cut it. Bryan wasn't sure if he had heard his mother correctly, or if he created the words himself in his mind. It wasn't possible that she was telling him that his former college roommate, co-worker, and best man was also his half brother. Bryan couldn't decipher what he was feeling inside. How long had his mother known that Wayne was his half brother? Did Wayne know that they were brothers? Questions continued to race through is mind. Everything that his mother was telling him sounded implausible. All the money in the world couldn't convince him that his mother was just finding out this information. Bryan composed himself and began to speak as calmly as he could.

"Momma, what's done is done and nothing can change the past. I'm just trying to comprehend a few things. I've seen Wayne's dad at least a hundred times. After all this time, you're telling me that I was looking at my father."

"Son, I didn't know things would go down the way they did. I honestly thought Gloria was dead since no one had heard from her in over twenty years."

"The secrets are out, mom. I just need to know how long you have known that Wayne and I had the same father."

"There were rumors, son, but I don't pay attention to rumors."

"I can't believe that's the only answer you have for me."

Bryan sat down at the kitchen table diagonal from his mother. He looked at her and wondered did she ever think that her answers and actions at any point were logical. He began to think back when he was a young boy and he had to help his mother dig holes to bury boxes and bags in the woods behind Jon Senior's home. His mom always told him it was a mystery game until he was old enough to understand differently. Bryan wasn't sure if his mom ever killed people, but he knew for a fact that his uncle had. Perhaps he couldn't blame his mom for her paranoia, lies, and insecurities. Her environment made her that way.

"Does he know?" Bryan asked.

"Who?"

"What do you mean who? Does Wayne's dad know he's my father?"

"If he does, I never told him. It was better that way at the time."

Bryan knew that his mother really believed in her poor decisions. There were two sides to every story, but in this case, there were four. Unfortunate for Bryan, half the truth was gone since both Wayne and his mother were deceased. He was finally exhausted by the entire situation and decided he'd leave the conversation where it was for now. However, an underlying issue that presented itself was the vengeance of Wayne's father for his son's untimely death.

On the way home, Bryan was in limbo about sharing his newfound information with Kayla. He wasn't willing to discuss his family's criminal past, but he also figured he should refrain from telling her that Wayne was his brother. Knowing his wife, she'd have questions even he couldn't answer. He made it his duty to make sure she was as worry-free as possible during her pregnancy. It was that moment that Bryan realized he was no different from his mother. He'd hide and manipulate whatever he had to protect his family.

Chapter 12

After overhearing Alex's conversation with his dad, Kayla was against visiting Bryan at his job. The last thing she wanted to do was possibly run into Alex and have him question her about the call. Kayla knew how to make up a lie, but she wasn't as witty when approached on the spot. She decided to pick up Nicholas from her mother's house and return home where she felt safe. Luckily, once she opened the garage, Bryan's truck was already there. She was reluctant to tell Bryan about his boss since he loved his job, but she knew she had to. She just hoped that her husband would believe her and not suggest that she was being paranoid or delusional.

"Bryan, we're home," she yelled, tossing her purse on the table.

Bryan came from downstairs and immediately gave his wife an intimate hug. Even though he was always affectionate, his long, drawn out hold made it feel like he had been waiting for someone to console him. She passionately embraced him, knowing that she too had been needing the comfort.

"Is everything okay?" She asked.

"Bae, there's been so much going on that I don't even know where or how to start."

"Well...just start from the beginning and we'll figure out together what we need to do in the end."

Bryan looked deep into his wife's loving eyes. He knew he couldn't tell her about the paternity test scam and bringing up Jesse was senseless. He grabbed her hand, walked to a chair, and sat her on his lap.

"I just found out that Wayne was my half brother and the person that killed him was my cousin, Jon Junior."

"What? How?"

"My mom had a beef with Wayne's mom, Gloria Dean when they were younger working the streets together. Momma said that Gloria tried to have her killed, which is why she retaliated by shooting her."

"What was the beef about?" Kayla asked.

"Momma said some silly shit about ranking. I personally think that they were messing with the same man, this man got them both pregnant, and my mom tried to kill Gloria in rage."

"Wow! That is crazy! How was this hidden all of this time?"

"Before Gloria died, she made some confessions on a letter that she sent to Wayne. My mom claimed that the letter was orders to have Wayne kill me."

"You can't be serious!"

"That was my same reaction."

"Why would his mom want you dead? For Gloria to even know about you means she had to have still been in contact with Wayne's dad."

"Perhaps, but I'm sure Gloria knew that my momma was pregnant when they both attempted to kill one another. Momma claimed she never even told Wayne's dad that he was the one who got her pregnant."

"Well…somebody knew something. Besides, every kid should know both parents unless he was a threat to your guys' lives or something. Maybe your mom thought she was protecting you."

"It's all confusing as fuck to be honest. I just don't believe after all this time that Wayne would try to kill me."

"Do you think it's possible that his mom put something in that letter that would have motivated him to try and kill you?"

"I... I don't know."

"Then again, maybe it was something in that letter that Wayne's mother had confessed, and Wayne had to be killed in order to prevent that information from getting out," Kayla suggested.

At that moment Kayla heard her phone ringing from her purse. She went to retrieve it and saw Dylan's number. Her heart quickly began racing. She knew she could not answer the call-in front of Bryan.

"Who is that, babe?"

"Uh...its Meg calling trying to make amends again. I guess someone went behind my back and told her I was trying to go to a private practice."

"Why is she so obsessed with you? Is there something you're not telling me?"

"You and I both know that Meg is completely off her rocker, but there is something I have to tell you," she said, reaching back into her purse. "We will be welcoming our little princess soon," she continued, showing him the ultrasound photos.

"Oh my gosh," he said, smiling as he hugged her.

"Are you slick disappointed?"

"What type of question is that? Of course not. She's already daddy's little princess. I can't wait to spoil my baby girl."

Bryan continued to talk about all the things he wanted to do for the baby. He started imagining trips to Disneyland, her first steps, and even what her first Christmas would be like. He got so into the conversation that he didn't even think about the baby being a newborn for her first Christmas.

Kayla was also enjoying the moment as she laughed at his silly baby gift suggestions. In that moment, everything seemed so fresh and renewed that Kayla forgot about overhearing Alex's conversation with his dad. After having dinner and putting Nicholas to bed, Kayla wanted to keep the mood going. She seductively urged Bryan to meet in their bedroom in an hour. Bryan readily agreed as he advised her that he'd be up after finishing his beer. About 10 minutes or so later, Kayla's phone rang again. Bryan ignored the first call, but this person was too persistent. He assumed it had to have been the same person that called earlier. His gut instinct was to answer.

"Hello, how can I help you?" Bryan asked.

"Hello, I'm sorry. I was expecting Kayla. This is Dylan Wright, Meg Wright's husband. Is she around?"

"I am her husband, Mr. Phillips. I am intercepting her calls right now, so how can I help you?" Bryan repeated.

"Well, it appears that your wife, my wife, as well as I have some unfinished business."

"What my wife and your wife have going on should never pass a barrier where we as men should get involved. I personally don't get involved with womanly shit. However, if you are saying to me as a man that you're already involved, then I'm also tagged in by default. From this point on, we will hash things out with one another as men, and not as our wives' husband."

"That sounds fair indeed. I definitely like to be clear on things as well, so just for my understanding; I want to be certain that there isn't a threat intertwined in your wording."

"It's Mr. Wright, right?" Bryan asked.

"Yes sir. It is."

"Okay...well, allow me to say this, Mr. Wright. The only thing certain in life for all of us is death. I go to work, pay bills, take care of my family, and make sure they have the things they need and most of what they desire. My family's happiness is what keeps me living even though I have a nonnegotiable contract with death. With this being said, Mr. Wright, may God prematurely forgive me if I cross the path of any man with the intent to harm my family. I hope that my response satisfies your uncertainty.

"Nice speaking to you, Mr. Phillips," Dylan replied, immediately ending the call.

Bryan wasn't quite sure what was going on, but Dylan had him fucked up if he thought he could handle any type of business with Kayla without going through him first. His assumption was that after Meg purchased the venue for the wedding, Kayla didn't want anything to do with her, so Meg probably felt used. He knew how strong-minded his wife was, so he figured that Meg had asked Dylan to get involved. Bryan decided that he wasn't going to tell Kayla about the call because he didn't want to ruin her mood or the chance of him getting some. Getting loving from his wife was hard to come by since she'd been sick throughout the pregnancy.

After showering, he gave his wife a full body massage starting with her shoulders down to her toes. He used sweet almond oil as he rubbed her skin while penetrating her muscles in circular motion. This was his strategy to accentuate the sensation. Towards the end of the massage, he licked his fingertips to sexually seduce her clitoris in order to increase her natural vaginal lubrication. He went in tongue and lips first. Her gratification was instantaneous. Putting her on top, he slowly eased himself inside of her, confirming that her moans were from pleasure and not discomfort. The moment felt perfect as his succulent kisses upon her lips had sealed the deal. He held her as they drifted into a pleasant slumber. It was an amazing end to a dramatic day. Needless to say, they were negligent to the fact that they should have revealed what they thought was best to conceal.

Chapter 13

The next morning Bryan went to the job site feeling liberated. Releasing his sexual frustration helped, but most of his freedom came from letting go of the past. It didn't make sense to stress about things he couldn't change. His mother's confessions weren't going to bring Wayne back or make up for them having absent parents. Besides, his mother would never tell him the whole truth, just her truth. It wasn't like Wayne's mother was around to contest it. He wasn't even going to ask his mother anymore questions about her past. He was even done with Alex's involvement with Jesse. He was only focusing on being a good parent and giving their children the childhood that he never had.

"What's going on, B?" Alex asked as he walked up to Bryan.

"Man, I'm just trying to keep my mind clear and focus on the positive. I have a little princess on the way."

"Congratulations! That's awesome."

"Thanks, man."

"Hey, I wanted to ask you if your wife mentioned anything about the call she made yesterday."

"A call? A call to who?"

"It's in my phone. It was yesterday evening," Alex said, showing him in his phone.

"No, she didn't mention anything. Did she call you back or something?"

"Uh, no. I figured she couldn't reach you or something, so I tried to call her back to make sure nothing was wrong."

"It was probably an accidental dial or little Nick playing with the phone."

"Damn…I didn't even think of that. Well, I'll let you get back to it, man. Call me if you need something," Alex offered, walking off as he made a call.

Bryan didn't think much of it either since Kayla didn't mention it. However, he did notice that Alex looked exhausted as if he hadn't had sleep in days. It was the same dazed look of the drug addicts he once served during his previous lifestyle. Bryan considered talking to him as a friend, but if it had anything to do with Jesse, he refused to get involved. He had enough problems going on without adding more to the pot.

Back at home, Kayla surprisingly woke up without any morning sickness. Her stomach felt tight as she looked down at her belly, which seemed to have grown overnight. She put on some fitted scrubs and headed downstairs to grab a breakfast bar. She thought about the wonderful night that she had with her husband, and then she suddenly realized that she forgot to tell him about Alex. After grabbing her phone, she quickly decided that it may not be a good idea to call him at work. She placed her phone on the counter and considered texting him to call her once he got a moment to himself. A few seconds later, she received a call from a familiar contact.

"Dexter?"

"Hey boo," he whispered.

"I am about to pass the fuck out! We thought you were missing or worse!"

"I am missing. I was kidnapped."

"What? Are you okay? Where are you?"

"You are asking too many questions."

"What do you mean I'm asking too many questions? I get a message that you were literally snatched up without a trace and now I'm asking too many questions?"

"Uh…yes. Sometimes you can be so dramatic, but I love you though."

"I can't deal right now, Dexter. You are going to give me grey hairs before my kids get the chance to."

"Whateva, boo. You know you love me, but seriously though. I have something extremely important to tell you, but I can't talk long, so listen. Meg hired someone to kidnap me and it was an epic fail."

"I am literally afraid to ask for further details."

"Well…you betta listen because you're gonna need'em. Turns out the kidnapper is gay, bitch."

"Huh?"

"Yes, bitch. My gaydar detected it right away and we hit it off. We are in love and we about to be paid. I can already feel the sand between my toes."

"Wait. I have to sit down because this is beyond my comprehension level."

"I know, boo, mines too, but that's not what's important and you don't have time to sit down. You can't go to work today, and you might need to leave your house."

"Why?"

"You don't have time to keep askin' all of these questions. I'm calling to let you know that Dylan plans on teaching Bryan a lesson by kidnapping you."

"That's absurd. Bryan isn't involved in this."

"Uh…he made himself get involved when he threatened to kill Dylan last night."

"What? Bryan wouldn't threaten to kill someone he doesn't know. Bryan hasn't even had a conversation with Dylan."

"Boo Boo, how did you become so clueless to everything surrounding you? They talked last night on the phone."

"I was up with Bryan all night last night, so there is no way they talked on the phone. Someone must be lying to you to get you to spread some false information."

"You need to check yo phone, honey, because I'm telling you that this man.... I'll have to call you later." He quickly whispered, ending the call.

This had to be the most bizarre thing Kayla had experienced since Bryan getting shot. She was relieved that Dexter was still alive, but as usual, he was too much to handle. Deep down inside, Kayla knew there had to be some truth to what he was saying. She then remembered that she had left her purse and phone downstairs while Bryan was drinking his beer. He must have been suspicious when she hadn't answered her phone. She looked back through her call log and there it was. Dexter's story was accurate. Dylan had been spoken to for five minutes and eight seconds.

Kayla's good spirits suddenly transformed into anger and anxiety. Had Dexter not informed her about Dylan's devious scheme, anything could have happened. She wasn't sure what she would do next. She could stay at home for the day, but she couldn't hide forever. Kayla headed back upstairs, grabbed a few of her and Nicholas's belongings, and headed to the garage. There wasn't a plan in place, but she figured she'd go over her mom's house with Nicholas until she came up with a strategy. Furthermore, it would be safer until she had time to talk to Bryan.

As Kayla put the suitcase in her trunk, she wondered what was it that Bryan could have possibly said to offend Mr. Wright. Kidnapping was a serious crime and what did he plan to do with her if he accomplished it? Bryan didn't know anything about the video or Meg's whoring around town. Still not coming to any type of logical conclusion, she got in the car and opened the garage door. Just as she was about to put the keys in the ignition, she dropped them on the floorboard. As she struggled to bend sideways to retrieve them, she was startled by a loud tap on her passenger window. A curtain of sheer fear overcame her as she looked over, clutching her purse. Dylan Wright stood next to her passenger door with latex gloves on, holding a shiny sliver pistol.

Chapter 14

"Kay-la," he called in a singing voice, "we have something to talk about."

Her predicament worsened within a matter of minutes. There was no telling how long Dylan Wright had been waiting outside for her. Dexter must have heard about the plot after it was already in place. She considered starting the car and smashing the petal, but surely a bullet would have penetrated her windshield before she could even make it halfway out of the garage. Kayla had no choice. Her only option was to comply with his demands. From her perspective, it didn't appear that he was there just to scare her or else he wouldn't have worn gloves. She had to try and alter his perception of the way he assumed she would react. She let down her passenger window and attempted to make him feel as if this was a casual encounter.

"Good morning, Dylan. What brings you over so early?"

Much to her surprise, it seemed to have worked better than she assumed it would. As he was still slightly bent over, Kayla could see his facial expression change into confusion as he looked down toward the ground. He placed his gun back into the holster and calmly walked around to her door. He opened it and politely asked her to step out of the car. She grabbed her purse as she followed his request.

"You won't be needing that," he said.

"Oh, okay. I didn't want my husband to find my purse in my car and assume something is wrong."

"How thoughtful of you," he responded.

"So…should I grab it or?"

"Kayla, what do you think this is? Something is wrong, and your husband should be very worried. It's obvious what's going on here, so stop acting oblivious to the matter at hand."

"I'm not acting, Mr. Wright. I'm looking at this encounter from a literal point of view. You haven't asked or forced me to do anything that I've objected to."

Her counter active approach seemed to have quickly annoyed him. It was almost as if he wanted her to be frightened. She thought about screaming for help, but she reconsidered. There was a possibility that Dylan just might have been heartless enough to shoot her dead in her own front yard. She figured she'd have a better chance by talking him down or negotiating if she went with him.

Dylan tightly grabbed her arm and escorted her to the black SUV that was parked out of view of the driveway. He took her over to the passenger side and waited until Kayla fastened in the seat before leaving. All she could think about was where nosey old Ms. Rose was when you needed her. As a matter of fact, where was anyone? Dylan was abducting her at a time when there seemed to be not a soul in sight. Kayla became overwhelmed with the seriousness of her predicament.

The drive was silent as Dylan carefully maneuvered through the traffic as if nothing was wrong. Kayla knew she had to do something, but she also knew it would only take a few seconds for him to retrieve his gun if she signaled for help. Without her phone, there was no way to message anyone. Had she not been pregnant, Kayla would have gotten out of the car and made a run at the red light. She took a deep breath as she thought out a few scenarios. Before making an erratic decision, she had to know where his mind was. She was done playing the nice card. She needed to decide her next move.

"I'm guessing this is about the video that I sent to you starring your wife." She finally said.

He chuckled. "You and your husband both have a terrible way of communicating with businessmen."

"Keep my husband out of this. You've never even met him."

"I don't have to meet him to know he is an arrogant asshole. The little bastard has no respect for his superiors."

"Well, I'd rather him be an asshole with no respect than an adulterous murderer."

"You know something, Kayla; I always thought you were a very vibrant and intelligent young lady. I figured you would excel to a point where you would even out do my wife, but that perception changed. You're not smart at all. I couldn't for the love of me figure out why you would send me a video of my wife slicing Jared's neck and think that I wouldn't try to protect her."

"I could think of more than a few legitimate reasons, but mainly because I was under the impression you were offering an award for anyone who could find your lover's killer."

Kayla noticed him grip the steering wheel tighter while clenching his teeth. She could tell he was getting upset, but that's what she wanted. Getting him out of his element would indubitably make him reveal his true intentions with her.

"I'm glad that you think this is one big joke. Like that little Kevin Harvard boy says, *laugh at my pain.*"

"It's actually Kevin Hart."

"It doesn't matter. My point is that laughter is the key to a broken spirit and you best believe, Kayla, we will have the last laugh."

"Do you wanna know something weird, Mr. Wright? My perception of you was different as well."

"Oh…how so?"

"Well, I always saw you as a refined gentleman with character. I was under the impression that you had everything figured out and that you were the one who kept Meg grounded. I always assumed that you were the solid one in the marriage. Do you know what I'm saying? I believed that you were the one between the two of you that built the foundation and kept the relationship stable. Then I realized that you're just as lost and as loony as she is."

94

"Kayla, no one has all the answers. While I am a man of many accomplishments, I am also a man of many mistakes. However, in my wife's defense, one can theorize that my wife was exceptional enough to string you along like her puppet for quite some time."

"That's not a compliment to her. I mean, you just said yourself I wasn't so smart. I'm also appalled that you would still characterize your wife as anything other than a satanic monster after seeing what she did to Jared. Not to mention that baby clearly isn't yours."

"You shut the hell up, Kayla. You are taking this too far. Besides, no one is perfect. People make mistakes. It's a great thing that she has someone like me to fix it for her."

"You are clearly delusional if you think you'll get away with this."

"Of course, I will. Meg told me about this mysterious person that you claim you sent the video to, which is why it was sheer luck that I had the opportunity of speaking with your husband last night. Evidently, you two seriously lack communication or perhaps he wears the skirts in your home. I called you to negotiate another deal; however, I discovered that the poor boy has no idea about what's going on. I was so elated that he wasn't the mystery person. I fancied by the time this mystery person finds out that your missing, my pregnant wife and I will be in Aruba."

"You and your mutt are a disgrace to human decency and you belong in hell."

"Lucky for us, that's not your decision. Besides, you're the one that video taped the entire thing. I guess that is what helps you get your rocks off."

"Hearing your wife explain how she use to suck Jared and every other black man off is what got me horny."

Kayla could see the veins flare up as his face turned red. He took his right hand off the steering wheel and backhanded Kayla on her left eye. Out of pure reaction she grabbed the steering wheel and jerked it left, crashing his side between a park bench and a light pole. No one in the vehicle was moving. The horn sounding off from Dylan's face being smashed between the seat and dashboard was a horrific scene that onlookers encountered.

Chapter 15

Bryan caressed his wife's head as he looked upon her resting body. He couldn't believe that this old man had the audacity to lay hands on his wife. Apparently, Dylan Wright had taken Bryan's promise as a joke. The investigators had advised Bryan that they assumed that Kayla was abducted from the home as she was leaving. The report from the next-door neighbor confirmed that a man had threatened her with a gun as she questioned him about being parked in front of the residence. The neighbor went back into her home and called the police as she watched the man force the woman in the car. However, the party in question had already vacated the premises before dispatch had arrived.

After carefully searching the premises, officers concluded that no one was present at the home. They found Kayla's purse with all her belongings including her keys that were still in the ignition. It wasn't long before they received a call about a crash not far from the area. After they arrived at the accident and surveyed the scene, they realized it was the same suspect they were looking for in connection with the abduction. It was their conclusion that Dylan Wright had attempted to assault her, losing control of the vehicle.

Bryan was undoubtedly furious when he heard the story. He had every intention to show Dylan that he was a man of his word. The good Lord was surely in their corner before Bryan could carry out his plan. Dylan had unfortunately succumbed to the injuries of the accident, but Kayla was alive, and the baby was healthy as an unborn could be.

Feeling dazed and confused, Kayla woke up in the hospital bed a few hours later with a serious migraine. Once she realized where she was, panic overcame her as she raised up and gently pressed on her stomach. She looked around and didn't see anyone in the room, which added to her anxiety. She was startled and relieved when Bryan opened the bathroom door.

"Hey beautiful wife of mine. How are you feeling?"

"I'm not sure. What's going on?" She asked, still rubbing her stomach.

"Don't worry, Sweetheart. The baby is fine and so are you."

"Why does my face and head hurt?"

"You were in a car accident."

"That wasn't a dream?"

Bryan shook his head. She slowly lied back and tried to recall what happened. All she could remember at that moment was a loud horn. The ringing in her ears seemed to have elevated the head pain. She told Bryan that she needed medicine and he quickly called the nurse. After taking the medicine, she was advised to relax as Bryan rubbed her hand. After a few minutes of silence, she smiled at him and fell back asleep.

*   *   *

A few months had passed, and things were pretty much back to normal. During the full investigation of the kidnapping, the detectives couldn't recover Dylan Wright's cell phone. They couldn't determine if he didn't have it on him or if a passerby swiped it up in the chaos. While it was no issue corroborating the timeline and the order of events with the neighbor, they couldn't substantiate the reason for the abduction.

Kayla didn't mention anything regarding the video in fear that she may be charged for withholding incriminating evidence. She told investigators that Dylan attacked her because she would not give him information about who his pregnant wife was having an affair with. Without any cooperation from Meg, that's all they could go by even though they made it clear that they were keeping the investigation open.

Despite the past mishaps, Kayla and Bryan we're doing awesome. Once she returned from maternity leave, she would resume the position of head of the department in Meg's position. After Dylan died, it seemed like Meg had disappeared into thin air. People claimed that she was so heartbroken that she had to move across the world, but Kayla knew that was far from the truth. Meg had gotten the insurance money for Dylan's death and went into hiding from Jared's murder. Maybe she thought she'd get away with it, but those types of transgressions will always follow her.

Bryan also received a healthy pay raise for his new position as part owner of Alex's landscaping business. Alex had explained that he always had his back even when he didn't have to. Alex had admitted to Bryan that he had a drug problem and would be going away for a while so he could get his life together. Bryan was at the least bothered by the fact that he was doing all the work while Alex was in rehab. Due to Alex's continual relapses, it was likely going to be that way for a while. Bryan was just happy that things were working out and even more elated when Floyd's paternity test came back negative. He knew that having Floyd to take his test wasn't the right thing to do, but considering the circumstances, it was the only thing to do. Besides, he was 99 percent sure that wasn't his child. His biggest concern was what Floyd may need in return.

Although Bryan wasn't on the best of terms with his mom, he still invited her over to see baby Bryla Iria Phillips. His mom cried when she heard the name. Kayla just hoped that everything would be good by the time she returned to work. Her plan was to have both moms helping with childcare duties.

Besides dealing with Dexter complaining about having to come back to work since his new lover was broke, Kayla didn't have any complaints of her own. She had learned, lost, and gained more in the last six years than she had in her entire life. She also confessed everything to Bryan and promised not to try to handle any other insane situation on her own. However, she didn't bother telling Bryan about the conversation she had overheard between Alex and his dad. Alex's demons were between him and his family, not her husband. Kayla was proud of their accomplishments and especially their healthy eight-pound blessing. Everything was wonderful for the time being.

The Author

"Thank you for taking the time to read part VI of Partially Broken Never Destroyed. I look forward to providing you with future entertainment that you will enjoy."

Feel free to enjoy the entire series also available on Amazon.

Thanks again for your purchase! Here are some additional books by the author.

Get More Books

Guides

Unleashing Essential Oils: With Extra Invaluable Beauty Tips

E-book Supplier for First Time Home Buyer

My Diet Your Diet Our Diet

Experience of Life vs. Expert Advice

Children Book

Little Cupcake's First Day

Novels and Novellas

Partially Broken Never Destroyed I, II, III, IV, V

Alyce Leaves Wonderland

Upcoming

The Doctor's Inn: Private Practices

www.ingramcontent.com/pod-product-compliance
Lightning Source LLC
Chambersburg PA
CBHW022042170626
46808CB00003B/1334